For dear Rick Margolis —K. B.

To Ai, whose name means "love" and fits her perfectly —G. B.

All rights reserved. For information about permission to reproduce selections from this book, write to trade.permissions@hmhco.com
or to Permissions, Houghton Mifflin Harcourt Publishing Company, 3 Park Avenue, 19th Floor, New York, New York 10016.

hmhbooks.com

The illustrations in this book were created digitally, using Photoshop and a Wacom tablet, with some hand-painted textures.
The text was set in Fairfield LT Std.
Jacket and interior design by Jessica Handelman

Library of Congress Cataloging-in-Publication Data is on file.

ISBN: 978-0-358-00422-6

Manufactured in Italy
RTLO 10 9 8 7 6 5 4 3 2 1
4500835524

Lost
and
Found

Kate Banks & Galia Bernstein

Houghton Mifflin Harcourt
Boston · New York

The wood mouse and the rabbit raced around the big bend in the forest.

"What's that?" said the wood mouse, stopping short in her tracks.

On a moss-covered mound lay a rag doll.

The rabbit moved closer to the doll and sniffed.

He knew the fresh, sweet fragrance of the forest after the rain and the scent of wild honeysuckle floating on the breeze.

But the rabbit didn't know this smell.

The otter poked her head out of her burrow.
She placed a paw on the rag doll's hair.
"What is it?" the otter asked.
She knew the feel of the rough, ragged tree roots and the soft, silky heads of the pussy willows by the river.

But she didn't know this.

The other forest animals gathered around for a look.

"It doesn't have a tail,"
said the hedgehog.

"Or a wet nose,"
said the white-tailed deer.

"And it doesn't like nuts!"
said the squirrel.

Along came the beaver, who knew the sound of the water
washing over the dam and the whine of the wayward wind.
"What's that?" he asked when he spotted the rag doll.

"We don't know," replied the rabbit.

"I don't know either," said the beaver,
"but I *do* know what those are."
The beaver pointed to a patch of
footprints leading away from the doll.

"Let's follow them," he said.

The animals wove in and out of the shady glade
and under a canopy of oak trees.

They kept going until they came to a meadow.

They had never been out of the forest before
and it was a little frightening.

But they were curious.

Before them was a wide stretch of gray.
"What's that?" asked the squirrel.
The animals knew the forest trails thickly
carpeted with leaves and the rounded path
of the moon across the sky.

But they'd never seen a road.

They cautiously crossed it.
On the other side was a house.
"What's that?" asked the wood mouse.
The animals had seen the eagle's
matted nest and the den of the
hibernating bear.

But they'd never seen
a home like this.

Suddenly, the door of the house flew
open and a child ran into the yard.

The child looked familiar. It
had brownish hair and dark eyes.
And it had floppy arms and legs.
It was wrapped in soft-colored
cloth.

"Is that it?"
said the wood mouse.

"Maybe,"
said the rabbit.

"I think so,"
said the squirrel.

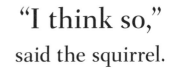

"Without a doubt!"
cried the beaver.

When the child returned to the house,
the animals tiptoed into the yard and placed
the rag doll on the swing.

Then they scurried back to the deep forest
where they went about their business.

But the next evening when the moon appeared,
the animals scampered to the edge of the forest again.
Across the wide, gray road in the window of the
house shone a bright light.

"What's that?" said the rabbit.
"It shines, but it's not a star," said the hedgehog.

They crept across the yard and right
up to the lit window.

Inside, the child was curled up in
bed with the rag doll, reading a book.

The child patted the doll's head and
kissed its cheek.

"I know what that is," said the rabbit, who knew the warmth of his mother's soft fur.

"So do I," said the wood mouse, remembering the sound of her mother's heartbeat.

"Me too," said the otter, who thought of her brothers tucked tightly in their burrow.

"I remember," said the squirrel, imagining the gentle touch of his father's paw.

"Yes," said the hedgehog, who fondly recalled sharing a meal with a friend.

"I know too," said the beaver, looking at his dear companions while the white-tailed deer smiled in agreement.

They had never seen a rag doll,
a road, a house, a child, or a lit
window . . .

but they all knew what love was.